Christmas Baubles

Christmas Baubles

A COLLECTION OF SHORT STORIES

Abby Ferns

For rights and permissions, please contact:
abbyferns21@gmail.com
ISBN (eBook): 9798227778468
ISBN (Print book): 9798227822130
Imprint: Independently published
1st edition November 2024

Edited by Carol Thompson
Credits: Licensed assets from FreePik.com

DEDICATION

To all those people who start humming Christmas songs as soon as the first leaf falls in autumn.

Other books by Abby Ferns

The elephant who couldn't trumpet

CONTENTS

Acknowledgement

My heartfelt gratitude to my beta readers — Tanya M and Marietta P.—who were instrumental in helping me shape the stories.
Special thanks to my editor, Carol Thompson, for fine-tuning my writing.

FOREWORD

If asked to select my favourite time of the year, I would unfailingly pick Christmas. My love for the season is a long-standing one and began way back in my childhood, when Christmas meant a beautifully decorated Christmas tree, sweets galore, and presents delivered by Santa Claus. The festive season also meant a steady stream of visitors to our home, and I simply adored the cheerful atmosphere that prevailed in my home during the Christmas season.

As I grew older, my vision of Christmas evolved from a love of the tangible aspects of the occasion into an appreciation for the sentiments—joy, hope, love, and compassion—this season embodied. Christmas is an occasion to put 'others' before 'self'.

I especially love the transformation that takes place in human interactions at this time of the year. People take time to acknowledge others in the street, and kindness and generosity are more readily found. Even the busiest people carve time in their full schedules to spend time with loved ones. For a brief moment, we focus on what truly matters.

Over the years, my notion of Christmas may have evolved, but the significance of the season remained the same for me.

The festive season has always felt like a reward given to us for all that we endure in the months that preceded it. All year round, we work hard to manage the life we have—academic, professional, family life—and then finally at the end of the year, we are blessed with a brief respite from this race for success to cherish what is important to us. The festive season feels like a balm to our bruised and battered souls that helps us rejuvenate our spirits just before we embark on a new year of adventure.

In keeping with my adoration for this season, I always start my countdown to Christmas a couple of months before the actual event. To be honest, I begin my countdown in September. However—my love for Christmas notwithstanding—this year I found myself craving the season even more than ever before. Primarily on account of a variety of factors across the world at large.

It's hard to ignore the news reporting the realities of wars, natural calamities, and man-made disasters. Then there is the negative sentiment—both economic and political—prevalent across most regions. And, if that wasn't enough, the toxicity in human interactions—hate speech found so freely on social media—would have a good number of people wishing for a hermetic existence.

And so, I began searching for the sentiments of compassion and hope that were seemingly missing in the world at large. I was seeking the sense of enveloping warmth that the Christmas season always offered me. My go-to for a boost of Christmas cheer—feel-good Christmas movies—failed to have the desired effect.

Thus, my collection of Christmas-themed short stories was born. I crafted stories based on myriad themes of loss, grief, discontent, disenchantment, nostalgia, kindness, and relationships that centered around Christmas. The stories are light-hearted and meant to warm your heart and boost your spirit. Perhaps they may serve to remind you that, despite the bleak period we are experiencing in life, there's always something to look forward to.

I hope I can spread some Christmas joy in your lives through these stories.

Wishing you a blessed Christmas!

Christmas in my heart

*A*s the opening bars of a popular Christmas song began playing over the radio, Samantha grumbled, 'Is there no other kind of music available at this time of the year?'

She flipped through the radio stations, trying to select one that didn't play Christmas music, hoping to find something pleasant to listen to on her drive home from the supermarket.

Christmas was about ten days away, and it seemed like the city had embraced the season wholeheartedly. From the festive décor in every store and window display, to seasonal food and drinks in every cafe and restaurant, to Christmas music serving as a constant backdrop in public spaces, you would need to be in a coma not to know what season was upon you.

Samantha found a radio station with a rather chatty RJ who thankfully wasn't playing any Christmas music, and she settled back to listen to some social commentary. However, her relief was short-lived as the RJ began talking about the 'Top 10' gifting ideas for Christmas.

Finally, giving up with a huff, Samantha turned off the radio and settled for silence to accompany her drive home. Luckily, she didn't have a long distance to go.

Gathering her many shopping bags, Samantha made her way from the basement parking towards her apartment on the third floor. She had more shopping than usual on this trip as she had purchased enough groceries to tide her over the next couple of weeks. She did not want to venture out when the shopping-crazy hordes were about town.

People went mad at Christmastime.

Samantha arrived at her apartment front door to find her elderly neighbour poised to knock on her door. 'Good morning, June. Were you looking for me?' Samantha asked politely.

'Oh, thank goodness you are back, Samantha.' June exclaimed.

'What's the matter, June? You seem worried.' Samantha commented as she opened the front door and beckoned June inside. She placed the shopping bags on one side of the entry hallway and gave June her complete attention.

'Please come in and sit down.' Samantha offered.

'I won't stay, Samantha. I came by to ask for your help.'

'No problem. What can I do?' Samantha was quick to offer help.

When Samantha had moved into this apartment building a little over two years ago, she had been a recluse. Keeping away from the neighbours and venturing out only for groceries. But June had looked past Samantha's obvious 'keep out' signs. She had initiated contact, claiming she wanted to 'introduce herself in case Samantha ever needed some neighbourly help.'

The friendly introduction was followed by weekly drop-ins, where June would come for mid-morning coffee or tea, bearing her latest baking success—cakes, scones, muffins. All under the guise of 'wanting Samantha's opinion' on the finished product.

Without being intrusive, June had gently coaxed Samantha to share her past. With June's help, Samantha took her first step towards reconnecting with people and stepped away from drowning in memories of a life that was no more.

While Samantha still led a rather quiet life, she was no longer a hermit. And it was because of June's kindness and generosity of spirit that Samantha readily offered help without even knowing what she had agreed to.

'I just received news that my sister had a fall and is in the hospital. She needs me to be with her.' June announced in a harried voice.

'Oh, June, I am so sorry to hear that.' Samantha responded, 'Of course, you need to be with her. What do you need me to do? Water your plants while you are away?'

'It's more than that, Samantha. Nate needs a place to stay while I'm gone. I'll be in the hospital with my sister, and I can hardly take him there. Could I leave him with you? It would only be for a couple of days.'

'Err,' Samantha was at a loss for how to respond. *Take care of a child?*

Seeing Samantha's hesitation, June carried on.

'There is no one else I can trust with Nate. It would

mean a lot to me, Samantha.'

Feeling small for hesitating earlier, Samantha replied, 'Of course, June. Nate can stay with me.'

'Bless you, Samantha. I'll just pack his things and bring him over.'

Shutting the door behind June, Samantha thought, *what have I let myself in for - taking care of a young boy?*

While she may no longer be a recluse, Samantha steers clear of children.

Being neighbours, naturally, she often ran into Nate around the building, but she avoided spending any extended time with him. The situation was about to change.

Samantha's chest tightened as memories long-gone but not forgotten assailed her. She made a slicing motion in the air with her right hand to ground herself. She wouldn't visit the past. *Not today.*

ooo

Barely an hour later, Samantha opened her front door again to June, only this time a grinning Nate accompanied her, carrying his school backpack and an 'Avengers' trolley bag.

June kissed Nate 'Goodbye' with instructions to 'Be good' and dashed off to the airport to catch her flight.

Samantha straightened her spine and invited Nate inside her modest two-bedroom home. She settled him in her spare room, which served as an office for her web developer business. There was a daybed in there and, while not ideal, it would have to do for Nate's brief stay.

'So, Nate, what would you like to do today?' asked Samantha. She was racking her brain for ways to keep an eight-year-old boy entertained.

'I was going to bake Christmas cookies with Nana June for our class Christmas celebration at school tomorrow. Could we still do that?' He asked.

Samantha groaned inwardly—*it just had to be a Christmas activity, didn't it? What was it about attracting that which you fear?*

But one look at Nate's hopeful face had her agreeing to his request. In the two years since she met him, she had yet to see him looking sad or forlorn, and she was not about to contribute to making him feel that way.

Fortunately, she had on hand the ingredients for the cookies, and soon, the aroma of sugar, vanilla, and spices filled the kitchen.

The memory of a Christmas past, when she had similarly rolled out cookie dough to the sound of Christmas music playing in the background, came to mind. The activity back then had been brimming with joy and unbridled childish laughter.

In comparison, the mood today was rather sombre.

Fortunately, Nate did not seem to mind it as he kept up a steady stream of conversation, telling her all about his school and classmates. He required little contribution from Samantha other than some sounds of agreement.

A couple of hours later, having pulled out the last batch of cookies from the oven, Nate had declared them a 'hit'. And buoyed by their success with the Christmas cookies, they added gingerbread to the menu.

Samantha had been surprised by how readily she had agreed to Nate's request for gingerbread but was glad she had done so.

Nate was clearly in his element and was going to town

piping funny faces and clothes onto the gingerbread men with the icing.

'Careful, Nate, or no one will want to eat them.'

'Don't worry, Miss Samantha. They are so yummy that no one will be able to resist them.' Nate proclaimed.

Samantha hoped Nate was right. She had not baked Christmas cookies or gingerbread for quite a while and was glad that she had not lost her touch.

ooo

The Christmas cookies and gingerbread were a big hit at the class celebration the next day, just like Nate had predicted.

'Everyone loved the gingerbread, Miss. Samantha,' Nate informed her as she collected him after school. 'My teacher said they were very creative.' He continued preening in the praise he had received.

'That's great to hear, Nate,' commented Samantha as she negotiated the after-school traffic. Samantha asked Nate how he would like to celebrate the start of his festive break from school. To which his reply was,

'Can we get pizza and watch a Christmas movie?'

Another Christmas activity.

She had gotten through the last activity but wasn't sure if she could sit through a couple of hours of make-believe Christmas cheer.

Perhaps she could plead work responsibilities and escape to her home office for a while?

'Sure.' Samantha replied flatly, though Nate did not seem to notice, engrossed as he was with the sights outside the car window.

ooo

'Won't you watch the film with me?' Nate asked when Samantha tried to make her escape later that day. She thought Nate was too engrossed in the film to notice her absence, but that plan was clearly a bust.

One look at Nate's beguiling face had Samantha give up her plans to escape and settle on the couch to view the 'Polar Express.'

Nate had clearly watched the film multiple times before as he mouthed the dialogue from memory. Yet, he sat enthralled by the movie playing out on the flatscreen TV.

It had been a long while since Samantha had last watched this film. Years ago, it had been one of her favourite Christmas movies. Despite that, Samantha found her attention wavering from the cinematic action unfolding on the screen in front of her to watching Nate enjoy the film.

His unadulterated joy in watching the film was more engaging than the film itself.

ooo

The following morning, Samantha placed a plate of waffles in front of Nate and moved the Hershey's chocolate sauce and maple syrup closer to his reach.

'Wow, Miss Samantha. I love waffles!' he cried as he poured chocolate sauce over the waffles and began eating.

Smiling at his delighted face, Samantha sat down to eat more leisurely as Nate peppered her with questions about different breakfast foods from around the world. Fortunately, Samantha had travelled extensively during the early days of her career and could field most of Nate's queries.

At the end of a lively discussion about his favourite book, Samantha asked Nate what he would like to do with his day.

'Can we visit the Christmas market?'

Yet another Christmas activity. Thought Samantha moanfully but did not have it in her to deny his wish.

After all, he had been easygoing all the while. No fuss or complaints while his nana was away. He had even done his fair share in the Christmas baking activity. She could hardly act like the Christmas Grinch in the face of that.

'Sure, Nate. Get ready, and we'll head out.'

ooo

As was expected, the Christmas market was buzzing with activity, with the school closed for the year. The market's sights, sounds, and smells were overwhelming to Samantha's psyche, but with Nate clasping her hand, she soldiered on.

Nate dragged Samantha from one stall to the next, pointing out everything from food and drinks to gift items and decorations. Clearly, Nate loved Christmas. But then, what child didn't?

It may have been years since she had visited the Christmas market, but she still remembered the joy on her little boy's face as he roamed the market. He could never get enough of Christmas.

Don't go there. Samantha warned herself.

Christmas was a season for family, especially children, and all the festive activities that centered around the family only reminded her of all that she had lost.

To combat the grief and sense of loss that Samantha felt when faced with all things Christmas, she tried to control her exposure to them through avoidance. She steered clear of shopping malls and community spaces in the weeks leading up to Christmas and ensured that her home was devoid of any festive symbols.

However, in his enthusiasm for the season, Nate was compelling her to face her fear.

It's only for another day or so. Samantha reminded herself. Then, *Nate goes back home, and I can retreat from Christmas.*

ooo

The next day, a call from June brought unexpected news. Her sister's fall was worse than June had expected, and she would have to stay with her sister for at least a week until they secured a carer for her. Being so close to Christmas, it was difficult to find someone reliable.

Samantha handed the phone to Nate for June to break the news to him as only she could. Walking to her bedroom for some breathing space, Samantha replayed the conversation in her mind.

Nate would be with her until Christmas. That meant that she could no longer ignore the festive season and would have to deal with it.

Samantha was not sure whether she could handle a festive celebration. The last two days had been tough enough, but a week of Christmas activities and a young boy was too much to ask of her.

She looked heavenward and asked, *Why me?*

Then it hit her; she was not the only one affected here. No child would want to spend Christmas away from their only family, and that too with a neighbour who lacked Christmas spirit.

What must *Nate* be feeling at this time?

Children deserve to be happy, especially at Christmas. Surely, Nate would not be happy with this arrangement.

Samantha realised she needed to put Nate's needs ahead of her feelings. Having strengthened her resolve, she stepped out of her bedroom to look in on Nate, sure that he would be upset following his conversation with his nana.

Sure enough, he was sitting on the sofa, rubbing a circle on the rug beneath his foot with the toe of his sneaker. He didn't look up when Samantha sat beside him.

'I am sorry, Nate. I know this is not how you would have wanted to spend Christmas.'

'It's okay, Miss Samantha. Nana June would be here if she could.'

'Is this your first time away from Nana?' Samantha gently probed.

Nate nodded his head sadly. 'I don't know how to celebrate Christmas without her.' He whispered.

Samantha's heart went out to the young boy, who had always displayed a cheerful disposition.

'Sometimes things happen outside our control, Nate, and we must make the best of it. It helps if we try to find something positive in the situation.'

'You mean I should be glad that I am not alone, and I have got you to spend Christmas with?' Nate asked, his eyebrows scrunched in thought.

Nate's perspective stunned Samantha.

While she had been trying to lighten his spirits, she had not expected that Nate would consider her a blessing. In her opinion, Samantha had done nothing to earn such kindness.

She may not have been mean-spirited, but her lack of Christmas cheer should have been clear to Nate by now. Yet, he had not voiced a complaint. He displayed an enthusiastic front throughout.

Then, she remembered every encounter she had had with Nate in the two years since moving into this apartment building. Even though Samantha steered clear of him, Nate was always cheerful and polite when they met. She knew he had lost his parents when he was young and lived with his nana following that incident, but looking at his cheery disposition, no one would guess the magnitude of his loss.

Children are resilient, but Nate had channelled his loss into a generosity of spirit that was truly endearing. Samantha realised there was a lot she could learn from him and, for once, she didn't resent his extended stay with her.

Where do we go from here?

'Miss. Samantha?' Nate urged gently, bringing Samantha back to the present moment.

'Sorry, Nate, just woolgathering.' Samantha replied, 'I am glad I have you for Christmas.'

Nate smiled brightly at Samantha's declaration.

'Though it doesn't feel like Christmas in my home, does it, Nate? No Christmas tree, lights, or decorations.' Samantha commented as she looked around her home and saw it through the eyes of a young boy. Although it was neat and clean, the house lacked warmth and personality. It looked rather boring.

'Those things don't matter, Ms. Samantha. Not really. So long as you celebrate Christmas in your heart. That's what Nana June says.' Nate replied sagely.

Samantha looked on, amazed at the maturity of an eight-year-old boy.

That evening, for the first time since Nate had stayed with her, Samantha suggested a Christmas activity to lift Nate's spirits. They watched 'Home Alone' and munched on popcorn, washing it down with some hot chocolate. Watching Kevin McAllister outwit two bungling burglars was strangely cathartic for both Samantha and Nate, as their shared laughter rang out in the apartment.

ooo

When Samantha went to bed that night, she thought about what Nate had said. *'Celebrate Christmas in your heart.'*

It had been a long while since she had celebrated Christmas in her heart. In fact, she hadn't celebrated anything since the fateful car accident that had claimed the lives of her beloved husband, Jeremy, and their darling son, Andrew.

Jeremy and Andrew had been on their way to the park, while Samantha had opted to stay home. She wanted to wrap and hide the Christmas presents they had already bought for Andrew. She did not want him accidentally stumbling across them weeks before Christmas and having to explain them to him. Being just 6 years old, he still believed in Santa Claus, and she would maintain that illusion for as long as she could.

Her world had been torn apart with a quick call from the local police informing her that there had been an accident involving Jeremy and Andrew. A speeding car had knocked them down, and just like that, her idyllic life had ended.

Jeremy and Andrew had been her entire world, and

being happy without them felt *wrong*. How could she be happy when they had been cheated out of their fair share of happiness?

However, the last few days with Nate had shown her that life was for the living, not for the dead. She would always carry the grief of losing her husband and son with her. But with time, the weight of that grief had lessened.

Instead of dwelling on what had been taken from her, she would try to focus on the love and happiness she had experienced with them.

Samantha decided to begin by opening her heart to Christmas, just like she had done when she befriended June.

She would start by creating a good Christmas memory for Nate to make up for his being away from his beloved nana. While Samantha could not grant Nate a Christmas with his nana, she would give him the best Christmas she could manage. She mentally listed everything she needed to do to get ready for Christmas.

Nate would be in for a surprise the following day.

ooo

The next morning, Nate walked into the kitchen and found Samantha humming a Christmas song as she prepared breakfast.

'You seem happy, Ms. Samantha,' Commented Nate. Her change in disposition was clear to him.

'I am beginning to celebrate Christmas in my heart, Nate,' was all she said.

A tribute to Nan

*T*he sounds of traffic and wailing police sirens from outside the high-rise apartment windows clashed madly with the Christmas music playing inside the stylishly decorated living room. The resulting cacophony would be unacceptable to most people, but Julie loved all aspects of city living, including traffic and noise.

On the rare Sunday when she did not sleep in, Julie would be found exploring the city and all its delights. The weather, language, culture, and lifestyle of living in the Middle East were in stark contrast to her childhood spent in the UK—yet Julie enjoyed it.

Well, she loved all aspects of life in Dubai, except the 50°C weather at the peak of summer. *Thank-God for air-conditioning!*

But this Sunday morning, Julie was sifting through storage boxes in her hall closet, determined to find her

Christmas decorations.

Where did I put the Christmas lights after I was done with them?

It had been two years since she had last used the Christmas lights and decorations, so she could be forgiven for not remembering where she had put them. But Julie was not one to go easy on herself.

If only I had organised the boxes properly. She thought.

I need to get the decorations up today.

While Julie was not known to procrastinate, her determination to set up the festive decorations stemmed from the fact that she had a deadline approaching at work. That meant putting in long hours until the project was delivered satisfactorily, because the work was sacrosanct. Everything else took a backseat.

Julie continued her search when she noticed a box that looked vaguely familiar to her lying towards the back of the closet.

Perhaps the lights are in there. She thought, pulling the box out and settling back to open it.

Julie pulled back the lid, only to gasp softly. Instead of finding the Christmas lights, as she had hoped, she discovered a box of her Nan's personal things.

Julie's mum had sent the box over, following her Nan's death in October the previous year. Julie had been too distraught at the time to deal with its contents and had put the box away without opening it. She channelled her grief over her Nan's passing into dedication to work, eventually forgetting about the box.

'Nan,' she murmured wistfully, and her heart clenched as an onslaught of memories hit her.

Julie's mind returned to her last conversation with her

Nan from more than a year ago.

ooo

'How is work and that young man of yours?' Nan asked.

'Work is great, Nan. I am swamped, but at least the bosses are recognising my work.'

'That's great, love.'

'As for Peter, we broke up. We tried, but it just wasn't working out, Nan.' Julie shared without rancour.

'Oh, *Julie!*' Nan seemed genuinely sorry to hear about the breakup. Fortunately for Julie, the pain over the breakup had eased with time.

'I tried, Nan. But it was an uphill battle. A relationship should not be a struggle, right?' questioned Julie. 'Just look at what you and Papa shared. Even Mum and Dad have a great relationship.'

'While your Papa and I had a good relationship, it wasn't without its share of struggles. Even your parents work hard at their relationship.' Nan explained, 'Everything worth having requires effort. You know that, Julie. When it comes to your work, you make such an effort. You need to do the same with your relationships.'

'Work is a priority, Nan. Now is the time for me to prove myself. A relationship will happen when it does.'

'Life is about balancing both aspects, Julie. If the balance is not right, it will make you unhappy.'

'Okay, Nan,' Julie sheepishly conceded.

'When are you going to visit us, love?' Nan asked, changing the topic.

'Soon, Nan. I am working on a couple of projects, and as soon as I can make time, I'll come visit.'

ooo

Only '*soon*' never came. Nan had been struck with a massive stroke and passed away in her sleep one autumn night shortly following their conversation.

For Julie, it was like being hit by a locomotive.

Nan—her 'rock', her biggest supporter, her confidante—was no more.

What made matters worse was that she did not even get to say "Goodbye". If only she had made time to visit more often.

The combination of guilt and grief had been overwhelming, and when her mum had sent over a box of Nan's things, Julie was in no state to deal with them. She had pushed it to the back of the closet, literally and figuratively.

Only now, the box was out in the glaring light of day for her to deal with.

Julie took a deep breath and decided to go through the contents. She began pulling out some of her Nan's personal items—old photographs of her Nan and Papa, photos of Julie at different stages of her life, birthday cards, and drawings that Julie had gifted her over the years. Nan had saved every one of them.

Julie found her Nan's favourite pendant among the contents, nestled in protective tissue paper. The one Papa had given her on their first wedding anniversary. It was a simple crucifix encrusted with tiny turquoise stones. Nan always wore it as a talisman. Julie was not overtly religious but decided to wear the pendant to feel a bit closer to Nan.

At the bottom of the box, Julie found a leather-bound

journal. *Nan's treasured recipe book.*

Julie lovingly brushed her fingers over the worn leather cover. This book was a mainstay on the shelf in her Nan's kitchen.

Julie flipped through the weathered pages, filled with recipes lovingly written down by her Nan, along with her notations and comments about each of the entries.

Within their circle of family and friends, Nan was renowned for her culinary skills. Nan was especially good at baking, and Julie had fond memories of afternoons spent at Nan's side helping her whip up one of her delicacies.

Julie remembered one weekend morning leading up to Christmas, when she was a teenager. She had entered the kitchen to find her Nan elbows deep in the dough she was kneading. A delicious aroma emanated from the oven, indicating that Nan had been busy since early that day.

'Why do you bake so much at Christmas, Nan?' Julie asked as she pilfered a tart cooling on the tray. 'We can hardly eat all of this.'

'I make all this to share with our friends and neighbours.' Came Nan's reply.

'But don't you get tired of all this baking?' Julie questioned.

'Not at all. I enjoy baking, and knowing my food brings people joy makes me happy.' Nan clarified, 'Food connects people, Julie. Never underestimate the power of food.'

Julie shook her head and went back to eating her tart. *The power of food indeed!*

Julie recollected numerous comments that she had heard during her childhood and adolescence from friends and neighbours about her Nan's baking expertise. *Perhaps Nan had won people over with her baking skills.* Julie chuckled at the thought.

On an impulse, Julie decided to pay tribute to her Nan this Christmas by baking one of Nan's classic recipes. It had been a while since she had last baked anything, but this felt like the right thing to do.

Julie leafed through the recipe book, trying to decide which recipe she could follow with her rusty cooking skills, and finally settled on the 'Twisted Spice Bread'. It was a soft, moist bread that was loaded with delicious spices. Julie fondly remembered eating this, slathered in honey and butter, on Christmas morning.

Fortunately, she had on hand the flour, sugar, and spices that she needed for the loaf. Julie had purchased a packet of yeast some months ago on impulse, planning to make bread, but never got around to it.

Better check the expiration date and make sure it is still safe to use.

Thankfully, it was!

Julie measured the necessary ingredients for the bread and began preparing the dough. As she went through the motions of mixing and kneading, Julie's mind travelled back in time to her childhood.

ooo

Julie's parents had demanding careers, which led to her spending her after-school hours at her Nan and Papa's home throughout her school life. Their home was as much a home to her as her own home was.

As Julie reminisced, she realised that Nan and Papa had played a starring role in her childhood. Whether tending to a scraped knee, learning to ride a bike or play chess, or dealing with boy troubles, Nan and Papa had seen her through them all.

Papa had passed away just before Julie could head to college, and she had deferred her admission by a semester to help her Nan deal with Papa's passing. Those shared months brought them closer in a way that Julie had not previously envisioned.

After completing her graduation, Julie moved in with her Nan while looking for a job. A severely constrained job market at the time had resulted in many months of unemployment. Julie then had to take the first job she was offered, which didn't pay a lot. Her Nan had been her rock through that difficult time, lifting her spirits and telling her that *'her time would come'*.

It did *eventually*.

After two years of struggle, Julie landed an entry-level position at a large design firm. There was no looking back after that.

To make up for lost time, Julie was determined to excel at her work and prove her talent as quickly as possible, which meant putting work first. However, prioritising work resulted in her skipping out on social activities—movie nights, drinks at the pub—and soon, that meant missing out on time with her family. Julie didn't travel back home to see her parents and Nan as often as she would have liked to.

Her ambition and subsequent success—while well-deserved—had come at a price; the price of human relationships.

While her parents hardly complained about her attitude towards her work—as they considered her to be *'cut from the same cloth'* as them—Nan never failed to remind her to strike a balance between work and family life. Julie's only response was to roll her eyes and shrug off the advice, thinking she had all the time in the world to deal with it later.

Now, as she kneaded the dough for the bread, she thought about the choices she had made to date. Julie loved her job but wondered if her single-minded focus on her work was the right way to approach her career.

Taking her eye off the ball could impact her career advancement, which was why she maintained her focus. In a competitive place like Dubai, when bosses felt an employee was not giving their *100%* to the job, they would shift their attention to another employee who was willing to *'give their all.'* Julie had not come this far only to falter now.

But perhaps she could ease off the pedal a little?

After all, she was more than just the *job title* she held.

The kneading of the dough proved to be therapeutic as Julie worked out her mixed emotions.

Soon, the dough was prepped and ready to be placed in the oven to bake. Between revisiting the past and reflecting on her life choices, Julie's mind was in upheaval. She felt an inexplicable need to connect with someone who would understand how she felt, and she reached for her phone to call her mum.

After exchanging pleasantries and catching up on the latest news in her parents' semi-retired life in Spain, Julie broached the subject of her Nan. Julie and her mum were finally at that stage where they could talk about Nan, without being choked with emotion.

'Mum, I keep thinking back to Nan's advice about balancing work and relationships.' Julie confessed, 'I ignored it, but now it feels like I should have listened to her.'

'Julie darling, your work ethic is admirable, but it won't be compromised if you make space in your life for more than just a career.'

'But you and Dad prioritised your careers as well.'

'Yes, we did. However, our respective careers did not take off until after you were born. It's only then that we went full throttle with our work.'

'Oh!'

'We could afford to do that because our relationship had a strong foundation for us to fall back on. Even then, we never took our relationship for granted. We were busy, but we made time for the important things in life.'

'Hmm' was Julie's non-committal response. It was true that while her parents worked full-time while she was growing up, they were always there for her *big moments* in life.

'Darling, make room in your life for *a life*. You don't want to hit retirement age and discover that you haven't lived *at all*.'

Julie signed off her call with her mum with a lot to consider.

Perhaps she could alter her focus a little to take in a little more of life beyond her job.

The oven dinged, indicating that the loaves were ready to be taken out. Julie pulled the loaves out of the oven and set them aside to cool before slicing. The kitchen was filled with the aroma of freshly baked bread, laden with spices. As Julie breathed in the aroma of spices that filled the kitchen, her heart felt much lighter.

ooo

As part of her tribute to Nan, Julie decided to share the Twisted Spice loaf with her colleagues at work. After all, Nan loved to feed people. What could be a more fitting tribute to Nan than sharing her recipe with people who would never have enjoyed her culinary delights otherwise?

And so, the following Monday, Julie took one of the spiced loaves to the office and placed it in the pantry kitchen for her colleagues to share. Whenever anyone had some food to share, it was placed on a designated table in the pantry for everyone to grab.

This was the first time Julie had brought something in to share. She hoped that her colleagues would like the offering.

They *loved* the spiced loaf.

Colleagues who had only ever nodded in greeting at her before now offered a quick word of appreciation for her generosity. Others complimented her on her culinary skills. Julie had never had so many people stop by her desk in a day or engaged in that many conversations that were not work-related. It was a refreshing experience.

Nan was right. Food does connect people.

ooo

Towards the end of the day, a messy-haired man, seemingly in his mid-30s, stopped at her desk and hesitantly introduced himself.

'Hi, Julie? I'm Simon. I work in finance.'

Julie smiled in response and acknowledged his greeting.

'I had a slice of the loaf you left in the pantry, and I just wanted to say "Thank-you" for sharing it with us.'

'It was my pleasure, Simon,' Julie said. 'I am glad you liked it.'

'It was delicious.' Simon said, 'It reminded me of something my grandma used to make. She passed away many years ago, and your spiced loaf reminded me of her,' he added softly.

'I am sorry for your loss, Simon,' Julie offered kindly, 'and sorry for triggering some painful memories for you.'

'Oh! You didn't.' Simon quickly corrected her. 'I mean, the memories weren't painful. It reminded me of good times.'

'Oh,' said Julie, a little touched that Simon would share something so personal. Julie surprised herself with her response of 'The loaf is connected to my Nan as well. It was her favourite recipe. She used to make it for us every Christmas morning.'

She then added. 'She passed away late last year.' Julie had never spoken about her Nan with her colleagues before that, but perhaps the mutual sense of loss she sensed in Simon urged her to do so.

'I am sorry for your loss.' Simon offered solemnly. 'I was very close to my grandma as well. She raised me when my parents passed away.'

'Oh!' said Julie, realising the weight of grief that Simon must have carried with him for most of his life.

Simon smiled softly in response to her comment.

They talked about their respective grandmothers and then discovered that they were both from the same county in the UK. Julie and Simon were in the thick of a discussion on the competency of their local football club when Julie's computer beeped a meeting alert message.

Sensing a mutual desire to continue their conversation, they agreed to chat further over a drink at the end of the day.

Julie resolved not to work late that evening. Baby steps towards *having a life*. She looked forward to an evening spent in good company and the possibility of a *new friend*.

Gently rubbing the pendant around her neck, Julie whispered, *I'm trying to find that balance you asked me to seek, Nan.*

The Secret Santa mix-up

*T*he atmosphere at "Grayson & Grayson" PR and Marketing consultancy firm was festive and relaxed, unlike the busy professional tone that was the norm.

The change in mood was undoubtedly due to the season. It was almost year end and company targets had been met and, in some cases, even exceeded. The following year's plan was ready to be set in motion as soon as the new year kicked in. Besides the pleasure derived from a successful year at work, Christmas was about a week away, and most staff were preparing for their festive break, which explained their jubilation.

'Christina, aren't you coming? It's time for the Secret Santa gift exchange.' My colleague Sue asked.

I pulled my attention away from my laptop and looked up at her. 'Let me just hit "send" on this email, and I will join you.' I replied, 'There. Done. Let's go.'

We started to make our way to the office lobby area, where a grand six-foot Christmas tree stood gaily decorated. At its base rested a heap of assorted presents of different shapes and sizes—the results of a Secret Santa campaign that our office team ran each year. Participation was optional for all staff, but it appeared that everyone had embraced the custom wholeheartedly.

'I hope I get something good from my Secret Santa this year.' Sue said, 'Last year, I got a water bottle. It was practical but not exciting.'

'I don't think *exciting* is the word that comes to mind when it comes to Secret Santa gifts. I will be happy if my gift is something useful.' I replied. 'Last year I received a body spray—for men.'

'Ouch!' Sue winced.

We both chuckled at that.

'Gather around, people.' Our boss, Barry, announced and went on to make a speech, thanking everyone for their hard work that year.

'I hope he keeps it short. I am dying to pee,' Sue whispered to me.

Thankfully, Barry did keep it *short*, and soon the gift-giving was underway.

Some moments later, I received a leather-bound journal, which I was rather pleased about. I had a secret love of stationery, and writing instruments were my favourite.

Sue seemed satisfied with the pine-scented candle she had received from her Secret Santa and had thrust it at me as she dashed to the loo.

One of the last names to be called out was my Secret Santa gift recipient, Mark. As he was handed his gift, I hoped he wasn't too displeased with my offering—a Fitbit. Mark didn't seem particularly athletic or tech-savvy to me, but they were a popular gadget, and most people seemed to want them—if not for their actual uses, then for the bragging rights of owning one.

Mark unwrapped his gift and exclaimed, 'Oh wow!' He then took out an old fountain pen from the gift box.

Wait. What? The question whirled in my head.

That was *not* the gift I had wrapped for him. The fountain pen was intended for my boyfriend of six months, Jason.

Slapping my head in frustration, I realised what had happened.

I got home late from work the previous evening and was rushing to get changed in time for my movie date with Jason. Before leaving for the date, I had to finish wrapping my gifts for Mark and Jason in time for today's gift exchange. In my hurry, I must have interchanged the gift tags.

Crap!

I had found that pen at a flea market when I had visited Lisbon earlier that year. It once belonged to a Portuguese writer of some repute. I loved the pen on sight and thought Jason would get a kick out of owning an item with some history.

There was *no way* I would give that pen away to a colleague. I *had* to get it back.

I went back to my seat and waited until Mark left his workstation. Sue had stepped out to grab a coffee, and I seized the opportunity to retrieve the fountain pen.

I casually strolled over to Mark's desk to avoid drawing

attention to myself. I kept my fingers crossed that I would not have to search his desk for it.

Luck was on my side. The pen was on his desk. I grabbed it and was about to step away from the desk when I came face-to-face with Mark.

'What are you doing here, Christina?' he asked curiously.

'I heard you received a fountain pen from your Secret Santa, and I just wanted to check it out. I like pens.' That excuse sounded rather lame, and I hoped Mark would buy my explanation.

He did!

'Take a closer look at it,' Mark suggested good-naturedly.

I opened the box and feigned amazement at the pen.

'It looks great.' I commented. 'A bit old, in fact. Wouldn't you rather have a new pen?'

'Not at all. So long as it works, I don't mind if it is old,' came Mark's gracious response.

Mark's response surprised me. Most people are attracted to shiny, trendy objects.

'It seems this pen has some history to it as well. There was a note below the pen explaining about it, I imagine,' Mark went on to say.

'You imagine?' I probed.

'Yes. The note is written in Portuguese, so I am not sure. I was about to use Google Translate for it.' Mark said excitedly.

'Translate what?' Sue asked. She had returned with the coffee and latched onto the conversation.

Great! An audience. Just what I needed. This was not going as planned.

'I got this note written in Portuguese, along with my gift,

and I need to translate it to know more about the gift.' Mark explained to Sue.

'Oh wow! That's quite an exciting gift for a Secret Santa exchange.' Sue commented.

Shut up, Sue. I didn't need Mark getting too attached to the gift. I needed to swipe it after all.

'Wait, did you say "Portuguese"?' Sue asked Mark, and he nodded.

'Just ask Christina about the note. She speaks Portuguese,' Sue added helpfully.

I wished Sue would stop talking *right away*. She was making matters worse. I groaned inwardly and hoped that my face did not display my inner thoughts.

This was not going well.

'Great. Here you go,' Mark said as he handed me the note.

'Err...it says that António Cabral once owned this pen. He was a Portuguese poet, playwright, essayist, and ethnographer.'

'Oh wow! That's some gift!' Mark gushed. 'I wonder who would make such an effort for me.'

'Maybe you have a secret admirer.' Sue added, grinning.

I glared at her. She was not helping here. I only hoped that Mark did not connect me to the gift.

'I need to track down my Secret Santa,' Mark announced.

'Why would you want to do that?' I asked. 'A *Secret Santa* is meant to be just that—*secret*.' I hoped that I had managed to dissuade him from pursuing the matter.

Mark was about to respond when his phone rang, demanding his attention.

Saved by the bell.

Putting an end to our conversation, we all returned to our respective work.

ooo

The following evening, Jason and I had a dinner date at an upmarket restaurant that had debuted earlier that year. I found it a bit too fancy for a midweek dinner, but Jason enjoyed dining out in trendy restaurants.

It's a happening place, as he liked to say.

I was heading home in a few days to spend the holidays with family, and Jason and I would not be together for Christmas. So, we decided to exchange Christmas presents over dinner.

Earlier that day, I had tried to retrieve the fountain pen unsuccessfully. Mark seemed busy with a report and barely stepped away from his desk. When he did leave the office for lunch, the pen was nowhere in sight.

Finally, resigning myself to the situation, I decided to give Jason the Fitbit.

Jason handed me an envelope, and I was intrigued by what it might contain.

Perhaps these were concert tickets? My excitement was palpable as I opened the envelope only to discover—*a gift card.*

Who gives his girlfriend such an impersonal gift?

'Perfect, isn't it?' Jason asked. 'This way, you can buy just what you want.'

'I would have liked anything you got me.' I said reassuringly. *Perhaps he was worried about disappointing me with a poor gift choice. That would explain the gift card.*

'You are a doll. But I hate the hassle of guessing what people would like as a gift.' Jason said. 'A gift voucher is ideal.'

'Getting to know someone's likes and dislikes is half the fun of gifting.' I tried explaining.

'Why bother with all that when a gift voucher suffices?' Jason said. 'A win-win.'

A win-win?

That had to be the most cringeworthy statement about gift-giving I had ever heard. But then, I shouldn't have been surprised. Jason had never displayed a sensitive side in all the time we had dated.

'My turn!' Jason exclaimed as he opened his gift from me.

'Oh wow! A Fitbit!' he gushed. 'That's just what I need. You know me so well, baby.'

Did I know him? I wondered.

'Now I am sure you will be on board with what I tell you.' Jason went on to say.

'What's that?' I asked.

'Well, since you are heading home for Christmas, I was thinking we should not stay exclusive over the holidays.' He explained.

Wait. What?

'It's just that there are so many events in the city over the holidays, and I can hardly go alone.' He continued. 'So, I think it would be best if we casually dated other people for the next few weeks while you are away.'

'Just so I am clear, you want us to see other people over the holidays to make *socialising* easier, and then you want us to pick up where we leave off—once I am back—in the

New Year?'

'Exactly! You *totally* get it.' Jason grinned. 'I knew you would agree.'

I had only asked for clarification, and he assumed acquiescence?

How clueless could this man be?

Then it hit me. Maybe I was the *clueless* one here.

Sure, Jason was fun to be with. He was outgoing, attractive, and had a successful career. He would certainly be considered a "catch" by society standards. But looking beyond these elements, we had rather different personalities. Our habits and tastes differed considerably.

While I firmly believed opposites attract, surely a relationship needed stable common ground to survive?

Maybe it was time to reevaluate our relationship?

This upcoming Christmas break appeared fortuitous.

ooo

The next day at work was rather hectic, with me having to wrap up my assignments ahead of my holiday. Finally, towards the end of the day, I was done with my work and was looking forward to my upcoming break.

'Christina, do you have a minute?' I heard someone ask, and I looked up to find Mark standing by my workstation.

'Sure, Mark.' I answered. 'What can I do for you?'

'It's about the fountain pen that I was gifted. I was hoping to talk to you about it.'

Ah, the fountain pen.

In hindsight, I realised Jason would not have appreciated the fountain pen as a gift. Certainly not in the way Mark seemed to appreciate it.

Perhaps the gifts had found their right owners. Providence?

'I have been asking around the office, and no one could

36

confirm that they were my Secret Santa,' Mark explained.

He investigated? Boy, was he determined.

'Why not just let it go?' I asked. 'You liked the gift, didn't you?'

'I did.' Mark confirmed, 'That's why I want to find my Secret Santa. I want to thank them.'

'I don't think they expect that, Mark.' I tried to reason out.

'Perhaps, but it's something I must do.' Came his response. He took a deep breath and asked, 'Are you my secret Santa, Christina?'

I was taken aback. *How had he arrived at that conclusion?*

'What makes you think it was me?' I asked, stalling my response. Perhaps by hedging, I could find my escape route.

'You said that you like pens and you speak Portuguese.'

'That hardly implies it was me.' I said, 'Many people like stationery. Lots of people speak Portuguese, too. In fact, Luiz from Finance speaks Portuguese. It might be him.'

'I did think so at the start. But I asked him already. And he said "no".' He explained. 'That only leaves you. Besides, I learned that you travelled to Portugal earlier this year.'

Make way for Sherlock Holmes here.

Finally accepting that he could not be persuaded otherwise, I sheepishly said, 'Yes. It was I.' I quickly added, 'In full disclosure, though, that was not meant for you. I had bought it for a *friend,* and I mixed up the gift tags.'

'Oh!' Mark said in disappointment. 'Would you like it back then?'

He was offering to return a gift he really liked. Was this bloke for real?

'No. You keep it. You liked it, didn't you?'

'Well, yes, I do. Are you sure?'

'Yes. I believe you appreciate it more than the person it was intended for.'

'I'd say they have rather *poor taste*.' Mark added with a smile.

I chuckled at that.

'Thanks a lot, Christina.' Mark said, turning to walk away.

He paused and said, 'Actually, I would like to thank you properly. Can I buy you a drink sometime?'

'You don't have to do that, Mark.' I said, a bit taken aback by the offer.

'I *want* to,' he stressed. 'It's the only way I have to thank you for the lovely gift. Just name the date and time.'

'Okay. Perhaps when I return from my holidays? In the New Year?' I suggested, warming up to the idea.

'That sounds nice. Happy holidays, Christina.'

'Happy holidays, Mark.'

Well, how's that for a turn of events?

I had previously considered the Secret Santa gift exchange as one of those mundane festive activities that most workplaces indulge in yearly. It didn't hold much significance for me.

But the gift exchanges this year led to an exchange of a different kind.

A tosser for a keeper? Who knows? The new year would tell.

Santa confessions

'*You went to a Christmas market without me, Mommy?*' I could practically hear my six-year-old daughter, Alice, admonishing me.

I chuckled as I pictured the pout on Alice's otherwise angelic face when she learns that I had visited a Christmas market. Alice was Christmas-mad, just like me, and any Christmas-themed activity was our favourite.

However, one could hardly visit Prague in December and ignore the Christmas markets. After all, they are *world-renowned* and attract thousands of visitors each year. I may have been in Prague on a business trip, but having successfully wrapped up my meeting, I reasoned that I had earned a trip to the Christmas market.

I had better get Alice a wonderful festive souvenir as a peace offering. I thought to myself as I walked towards the Old Town Square, which held one of Prague's two main

Christmas markets.

The square sat amidst a backdrop of historic buildings that mixed medieval, gothic, and Baroque style architecture, creating a stunningly atmospheric effect. Peter, my husband, would love the architecture of this city.

In the centre of the square stood a towering Christmas tree that was easily over twenty metres tall. It was wonderfully decorated and quite breathtaking. Coupled with the angelic voices of a childrens choir singing Christmas Carols nearby, the overall effect was almost magical.

A child's version of paradise.

I decided then and there to return to Prague the following Christmas with Peter and Alice. They would love it.

All around the square were brightly decorated wooden stalls selling a variety of items. The aroma of warm spices drew my attention to a stall selling mulled wine, and I treated myself to a cup as I walked around the market trying to take it all in.

The cold winter air was brimming with a bouquet of aromas, each fighting for dominance. The smell of roasted chestnuts, fresh gingerbread, and meats being grilled over an open fire clashed madly without being cloying.

Hearing metal being pounded, I stopped by a blacksmith displaying his craft as he hammered out heated metal to forge a tool—a first for me. There was certainly something for everyone at the Christmas market.

The market was teeming with people, as was expected for this time of year, and it didn't take me long to grow tired of the constant jostling as people browsed the market.

After having my fill of the Old Town Square market, I

made my way towards Wenceslas Square, which held the second of the two big Christmas markets. I passed a horse-drawn carriage ferrying people around town and added this to my wish list of activities for a future visit to the city.

Feeling peckish, I bought a Trdelnik, a local delicacy, to nibble on the way. The Trdelnik, also known as 'Chimney cake', is made of rolled dough that is spit-roasted and dusted with sugar.

As I took my first bite of the Trdelnik, the flavour of cinnamon exploded in my mouth.

This is scrumptious! I thought as I munched on the cake. *Absolutely addictive!*

Wenceslas Square was less atmospheric than Old Town Square and seemed to cater more to shoppers. The stalls here sold traditional handicrafts—handcrafted Christmas ornaments, trinkets, candles, toys, and embroidery. Judging by the offerings of the two markets, Prague was clearly a haven for lovers of all things Christmas.

I continued my amble through the market when suddenly my gaze fell upon a Santa Claus figurine. It made me stop in my tracks, and I stepped towards the stall for a closer look.

The Santa figurine was carved out of wood and about 18 inches tall. Wearing a long red velvet robe and hat with faux fur trimming, the Santa figurine carried a sack in his hand and had a soft, flowing beard that begged to be stroked. His blue eyes were kind and wise.

It was uncanny how similar it was to the Santa figurine that my parents had when I was a child. I had never seen another like it before.

I looked around the stall and realised there was only one

of its kind. *Indeed, this was providence.*

I seized the opportunity and bought it immediately.

Ecstatic with my find, I explored the market for more treasures. After much searching, I finally settled on a doll dressed in traditional Czech clothing. It was unlike anything we would find back home, and Alice would simply love it.

Armed with my purchases, I made my way back to the hotel.

Once in my hotel room, I unwrapped the figurine and marvelled at the find. It was an exact match for the one from my childhood—the one that stood on my parents' living room mantel all through my childhood.

While the Santa figurine was lovely, it meant more than a mere trinket to me. After all, the figurine from my childhood had been the recipient of my first heart-to-heart talk and had led me to realise the value of the act of confession.

I gently brushed my fingers across its surface, and my mind reminisced about Christmas when I was a little girl of five years.

ooo

It was early December, and the festive season had well and truly begun in our home. A wreath hung on our front door; coloured lights were strung up all around the house; a beautifully decorated Christmas tree stood tall in the corner of the living room; and the statue of Santa Claus sat on our mantle as always.

Our preparations were not just limited to festive decorations. The pantry shelves were chock-full with a variety of delicious Christmas treats—tarts, cakes, and biscuits—for our expected visitors over the festive period. I could not wait to lay my hands on these delicacies, but my younger brother Josh and I were not allowed to eat any of these treats until Christmas Eve.

This was grossly unfair—to my way of thinking. *Why make sweets if you can't eat them?*

So, my ingenious little mind had devised a plan to liberate some of these goodies for Josh and me.

I peeked out of the playroom and, hearing no sounds of adults around, I beckoned Josh to follow me to the pantry.

We made it to the pantry without being detected—*lucky us!* Grabbing a small stool, I climbed upon it and retrieved the box of biscuits from the shelf above. We grabbed a couple of biscuits each, gleeful at our success.

I turned to place the box back on the shelf and, excited at a successful mission, overbalanced on the stool. Terrified of falling off the stool, I grabbed the nearest shelf to right myself and accidentally knocked over a mixing bowl, which fell to the floor and broke.

I scrambled off my perch and stared in horror at the mixing bowl, which was now in pieces on the floor.

I had broken Mum's mixing bowl. *Oh dear!*

And not just any mixing bowl, but her *favourite* one, which Grandma had given her.

What was I going to do?

I was going to be in so much trouble.

There was only one thing to do—*escape.*

I grabbed Josh's hand and dragged him back to the playroom.

'Josh, you must not tell Mum about what we just did. The biscuits or the bowl. Okay?'

Josh nodded happily in agreement. He was three years old, and he did everything I asked of him, so I knew he would not say a thing.

Would Mum see the broken bowl and figure out I had broken it?

I waited anxiously for her angry cry and was mildly surprised when the minutes ticked by, and nothing happened.

Perhaps she was waiting to tell Dad about it when he came home from work? He would be so upset with me.

That night at dinner, I prepared for the inevitable scolding, and sure enough, Mum mentioned the broken mixing bowl to Dad.

That was it!

Surprisingly, I heard Mum say, 'I should have been more careful with it…'.

So, Mum had *not* figured out that I was responsible?

Whew! I breathed a sigh of relief.

My relief was short-lived though. As I was tucked up in bed that night, a thought occurred to me. My mum may not have known what I had done earlier that afternoon, but surely Santa would have known. Mum had told me that Santa knows *everything* that children get up to.

What if Santa puts me on the *naughty list?*

Oh, the horror! No presents for Christmas.

I felt terrible about that. This was turning out to be a *bad* Christmas.

Could I do something to fix it?

Maybe I could try talking to Santa and explain what happened. But how would I reach Santa?

A letter would not get to him in time, and I would also have to explain to my mum why I needed to send a second letter to Santa. *What to do?*

And then I remembered that we had a Santa figurine in our home. Surely, this figurine had some connection to Santa Claus, just like the Santa Claus at the Christmas grotto in the centre of town. He was not the 'real Santa' but could pass a message to Santa.

With my mind made up, I waited until my parents went to bed, and I snuck out of my bedroom. I tiptoed my way to the living room, crept up to the Santa figurine, and whispered, 'Hi Santa, it's me, Becca. Mum says that you know everything that children do. So, you know what happened this afternoon. I just wanted to tell you that it was an accident. I didn't mean to break the bowl. So please don't put me on the "naughty list". I would really like a present for Christmas.'

I went to bed that night, hoping that my talk with Santa had resolved the matter.

The following day, however, another horrid thought occurred to me.

What if Santa considered Josh to be naughty, too?

After all, he had also participated in the mission. By that logic, Josh might not get any Christmas presents either.

That simply would not do!

Josh was a wonderful brother who deserved a Christmas present, so I returned to the Santa figurine for round two of my heart-to-heart talk.

'Hi Santa, it's me, Becca, again. I just wanted to say that the broken bowl was my fault. Josh didn't do anything, so please don't put him on your "naughty list". He is a good boy and deserves a present for Christmas.'

I paused and added, 'I hope you can give me a Christmas

present too. But I'll understand if you don't.'

With my speech done, I decided to put the incident behind me and carry on as before. To my chagrin, I was not over the incident, as I had thought.

Over the next few days, an uneasy feeling crept over me, as if something wasn't quite right. I tried distracting myself with play and other activities, but the unease persisted.

Then, to my horror, I began to lose my Christmas cheer. None of the festive activities I had previously enjoyed made me happy.

This went on for days until I finally decided to tell my mum how I was feeling. She always had a fix and would make me feel better.

So, that night, as she tucked me in bed, I told Mum that I was feeling *bad*.

She asked how long I had been feeling that way, and I had no recourse but to tell her it had started with my stealing the biscuits and accidentally breaking the mixing bowl.

'Do you know why you are feeling bad?' Mum asked.

I shook my little head in denial.

'It's because you did something wrong and instead of telling me about it, you kept it from me.' She gently explained. 'Secrets can be rather heavy, and we grow tired of carrying their weight.'

'I was afraid that you would scold or punish me for what I had done.' I sheepishly admitted.

'I would have been upset, but I would not have punished you for an accident.' Mum declared.

'Sorry, Momma.' I said, 'I won't do it again.'

'That's good.'

'Momma, there is something else...' I trailed off.

My mum raised her eyebrows at that.

'Will Josh and I be on Santa's "naughty list"?' I asked with trepidation.

'Don't worry, pet. I will make sure Santa knows not to put you on the list.' Mum confirmed with a smile. 'But you'd better watch your behaviour next time.'

'I will. I promise.'

I went to bed that night, finally at peace with the broken bowl incident.

To my delight, I discovered that I was back to my old self the following day. My Christmas spirit had returned just in time for Christmas, too.

ooo

As I roused myself from my reverie, I became aware of my surroundings and the weight of the figurine in my hands.

Santa Claus plays an important role at Christmas for all young children, being the magical bearer of gifts. That Christmas when I was five years old, Santa came bearing a gift for me as well; however, it was a gift of a different kind. Instead of a toy, Santa gave me a lesson. A lesson that I carried with me for the rest of my life—confessions are good for the soul.

Gazing upon the Santa figurine, I realised that perhaps it was time for that lesson to be passed on from mother to daughter. It wasn't too early to teach Alice about the benefits of an honest confession.

I wondered what my husband, Peter, would make of that?

Finding Christmas

Stephen tugged the woolen cap that sat on his head a bit lower and continued his daily walk. It was the first week of December, and the morning air had a real bite. The temperature was in the single digits, but the cold weather hardly bothered Stephen. He found it exhilarating, and the cold weather had not caused him to miss his morning walk in years.

There were a few people out on the street at this hour, walking their dogs. Being a Saturday morning, people were likely having a lie-in following a busy week at work.

Stephen usually enjoyed taking in the sights and sounds of the neighbourhood waking up as he strolled along the quiet streets around his home. However, this morning, the sensory experience escaped him. Stephen was rather distracted; his mind kept replaying the conversation he had with his daughter, Sara, the previous evening about his grandson.

'Dad, Danny is unlike his usual self. He has been rather morose. Something seems to be troubling him, but I don't know what.' There was an underlying note of worry in Sara's voice.

'Have you tried asking him about it?' Stephen queried, surprised to learn of the change in Danny's disposition. Danny was a kind and loving boy who, fortunately, showed no signs of trauma from his parents' divorce back when he was five years old.

'Yes, Dad, but he is being evasive and says that nothing is wrong.' Sara answered in exasperation.

'What can I do to help?' Stephen offered.

'Could you try talking to him when he comes over tomorrow? You guys are close. Maybe he might tell you what he is shy or afraid to share with me,' Sara suggested.

'Don't worry, love. I'll get to the bottom of the matter and let you know,' Stephen assured her, and ended the call.

ooo

Since Sara's divorce, Stephen had stepped in as a father figure to Danny and his younger sister, Chrissy, to fill in the void left by their absentee father. He adored his grandchildren and would not watch from the sidelines while his grandson was troubled.

Checking the time on his wristwatch, Stephen retraced his steps back home. He had just enough time to freshen up and have his breakfast before Danny's arrival. Danny came by dutifully every Saturday morning to help Stephen around the house and join him on his grocery run.

After finishing their chores, the duo would sit down and have a catch-up or play a board game or two. Stephen looked forward to their weekly visits.

ooo

Later that morning, Stephen and Danny were halfway through their grocery run when Stephen started to pick up on Danny's mood.

Danny had walked past the bedecked Christmas tree at the storefront, barely noticing it. The displays of festive treats around the store, meant to entice children, did not even merit a second glance from Danny. For a boy who was Christmas-crazy, this was unusual behaviour.

The cheery Christmas music and festive decorations usually drew a comment or two from Danny, but this time, they failed to make an impact. Danny was unusually quiet, practically dull.

There is definitely something troubling the boy! Stephen thought, but he decided to wait until they got home to find out what was wrong.

ooo

Back home with the groceries put away, Stephen and Danny settled at the small kitchen table for a snack. Stephen decided to start trying to figure out what was bothering Danny and chose to begin with the biggest factor in Danny's life.

'How is school these days, Danny?'

'It's fine, I guess,' came Danny's response as he traced a pattern on the tabletop with his finger.

'Just *fine?* I thought you liked school.' Stephen asked.

'I *do* like school. There is just not a lot happening at school these days. Probably because of the Christmas break that's coming up.' Danny responded, bored.

Stephen nodded in understanding. He then asked about Danny's teachers and friends, but could not identify a problem in any of those areas.

Stephen then decided to try another questioning route. 'You must be excited for Christmas then, huh?'

'I guess, Grandpa,' was Danny's lackluster reply.

'You guess?' Stephen was surprised at Danny's tone. Danny would usually start counting down the days until Christmas as soon as school began in September.

'Well, I mean, it's nice to get a break from school and homework. Plus, there are Christmas presents to think of,' Danny clarified.

'I sense a *but* here.'

'Well, the Christmas stuff is not as exciting as before.' This drew a raised eyebrow from Stephen, which went unnoticed by Danny, who went on to say, 'Maybe I have outgrown Christmas.'

'*Outgrown Christmas?*' asked Stephen incredulously.

'Yeah, it feels that way,' Danny stated in a resigned tone.

'What makes you say that?'

'Well, I am not looking forward to Christmas like Chrissy is. She is excited about Santa and her presents. She even gushes over the Christmas tree and all the decorations.'

'Being six years old, I expect those things still excite Chrissy, just like they excited you at that age. But I doubt that you have outgrown Christmas. You have likely outgrown the idea of Christmas that you were used to.'

Danny grew thoughtful at Stephen's response.

'Does Christmas change as we grow up?' Danny asked.

'Christmas remains the same. It's our vision of Christmas that changes.'

'How so, Grandpa?'

'Let me ask you this,' Stephen countered Danny's question. 'What comes to mind when you think of Christmas, Danny?'

Danny thought about it momentarily and then answered, 'Christmas tree, lights, decorations, Christmas music, hot chocolate, Christmas cookies, Santa Claus, presents.'

'Okay. All these elements of Christmas are still available and made you happy until recently, right?' Stephen asked, to which Danny nodded his reply.

'So, then what changed this year?'

'It just feels like there should be something more than just this stuff.'

'And by seeking more than this *stuff*, you know that your vision of Christmas has changed.'

'Okay,' Danny commented thoughtfully.

After a moment of quiet reflection, Danny asked, 'Now that I know my vision of Christmas has changed, what can I do about it?'

'Ask yourself what you want Christmas to mean.'

Danny looked puzzled at this suggestion, so Stephen went on to explain.

'The festive season is an emotional experience, involving feelings of joy, hope, generosity, and compassion.' Stephen clarified. 'What feelings do you want to experience this season?'

'Could I have them all?' Danny queried in a typically childlike fashion, belying his ten years of age.

Stephen chuckled and replied, 'Sure, you can. You just need to put in more effort to enjoy them all.'

'More effort?' Danny puzzled,

'If you want more out of Christmas, then you need to put more effort into creating a Christmas experience.'

'How do I do that, Grandpa?'

'Once you know what emotions you would like to experience this Christmas, you can get started on thinking of what actions you can take to bring about those emotions. Then simply work on executing them.'

'Hmmm... I'll need to search online for some inspiration.' Danny responded, seemingly glad to have something to work on. 'I'll do that when I get home.'

'You don't need to ask *Google* for ideas, Danny.' Stephen shook his head. 'You children nowadays!'

'Then where will I find answers, Grandpa?'

'How about I share a story with you for inspiration?' Stephen proposed, 'It's about how we would celebrate Christmas when I was a child.'

'Every year, as part of our Christmas preparations, my parents would make Christmas baskets for the families in our community who needed a little extra love and support.'

'What did you put in the baskets, Grandpa?' Danny asked, intrigued by the idea.

'We used to put jams, biscuits, cakes, sweets, some toys...things people would consider treats or luxuries at that time. My mum would make a list of the families in need and what they needed. She would then build the baskets according to each family's needs.'

He paused and continued, 'My sister and I used to love helping her pack the baskets. Our home was *"Santa's*

Workshop", and my sister and I were his *"Little Helpers"*—my mum used to say.'

Stephen had a faraway look on his face as though he had travelled back in time to a Christmas in his childhood.

'What then, Grandpa?' Danny prompted.

'Then on Christmas Eve, all four of us would visit every one of those families and present them with a Christmas basket each.'

Stephen paused, as if recalling a memory. 'I still remember people's faces when they received the baskets. Their faces would light up with the biggest smiles. It was great to see that. It was even better knowing that I had played a part in putting that smile on their face. No present could ever match that feeling.'

'My parents made me realise that it truly was better to give than to receive. And that was especially true at this time of the year.' Stephen concluded his story.

'Thanks for sharing that story, Grandpa,' said Danny as he grew thoughtful.

ooo

Later that day, as Danny made to leave for home, he said to Stephen, 'Grandpa, I was thinking about what I could do to find those Christmas feelings you talked about.'

'Okay. Any ideas?'

'How about if I made a list of all the people in my life and looked at what they needed? Then, I could think about what I could do to fulfil those needs.' Danny suggested. 'Do you think that could work?'

'That's a great idea, Danny. Why don't you get started on it right away?'

Danny's eyes lit up at Stephen's confirmation.

'Will you help me work out the plan once I get the list done?' Danny asked.

'Of course, I will,' Stephen promised.

'Thanks, Grandpa. I can't wait to get started.'

Danny's excitement was palpable, his demeanour a far cry from the unenthusiastic boy earlier that morning.

ooo

A week later, Danny was back at Stephen's home, but this time he was rather exuberant.

'Grandpa, I made that list we talked about, so can I share it with you now?'

'Certainly, Danny.' Stephen responded as he settled down on the couch, ready for a lengthy discussion.

'Well, first on the list is *mum*, and as she is always so busy with office and housework, I thought that I could help with some chores around the house to make things easier for her.' Stephen was pleased and proud of Danny for putting his mother first on the list of people to help.

'Then, there is Chrissy. She was gifted rollerblades for her birthday and wants to learn to use them, but Mum is too busy to teach her. I thought that I could help Chrissy learn how to rollerblade.'

Stephen nodded at this suggestion, so Danny continued.

Danny went on to list his best friend, next-door neighbour, and teacher, with creative ideas of how he could be a help to them. With each name mentioned and the corresponding idea of help, Stephen's heart swelled with pride at Dany's thoughtfulness.

'Just one person is missing.' Danny stated softly, clearly

feeling bad about the omission.

'Oh! Who's that?' asked Stephen.

'You, Grandpa,' Danny admitted, as if it was obvious.

'You don't need to worry about me, Danny,' Stephen said, touched that Danny had considered him as well. 'I don't need anything.'

'Surely there must be something...' Danny persisted.

Realising how keen Danny was on including him in his list of recipients, Stephen said, 'Well, if you are adamant, how about you and I go on a hike in the woods outside town? It's been years since I have been on a hike, and I could do with the company.'

Danny considered the suggestion and nodded. 'Done.'

The duo then went on to fine-tune Danny's plans to *help others* over the festive season. It was evident by the end of their conversation that Danny was back to his cheerful self.

Stephen was glad that he was able to get to the bottom of Danny's uncharacteristic behaviour from earlier—disenchantment. By shifting Danny's attention away from the materialistic aspect of Christmas and towards the sentiments that the festive season embodied, Stephen had reignited Danny's love for Christmas.

The lesson that Stephen had learned as a child was true even today—it truly was better to give than to receive.

About the author

Abby Ferns was born in Bombay, India, and studied English literature in college. After completing her education, she moved to Dubai to pursue a career.

Throughout her demanding corporate career, her creative outlet was writing stories, which she scribbled away in journals, hoping to publish them someday.

A bend in the road at the age of 40 had her reevaluate her life choices. She finally mustered up the courage to pursue her dream of becoming a writer, and 'The Elephant Who Couldn't Trumpet' is her first published children's book.

She now lives in Portugal, where she is dreaming up her next story.

Other books for young readers

The elephant who couldn't trumpet

Eddie the Elephant has a very important role in the upcoming Spring Parade at Bluebell Woods. He has to trumpet loudly to lead the parade through the woods.

The only problem was - Eddie could not trumpet.

An elephant who could not trumpet? How can that be?

Follow Eddie's attempts to fix his problem in time for the upcoming parade.

Author's note

Thank you for buying this book and supporting
independent authors.
Now that you have finished reading the story, it would
mean the world to me if you left your honest thoughts
about it on your preferred retail platform.

— Abby Ferns